Sam's Story

Children Trying to Understand PTSD

C. L. Fontaine

Illustrated by Dwight Nacaytuna

To order additional copies of this book, contact:
Xlibris
1-888-795-4274
www.Xlibris.com
Orders@Xlibris.com

Sam's Story

Children Trying to Understand PTSD

C. L. Fontaine

Illustrated by Dwight Nacaytuna

Thank you,

Robert D. Ruplenas and

Karen F. Emery

Contents

Introduction

Sam's story is a fictional account of a young child's attempts to understand his dad's PTSD. His mother helps him by explaining it as well as she can, but in the end, Samuel and a newfound friend come to three conclusions: (1) PTSD is not their fault, (2) the children cannot change or fix PTSD, and (3) their parents love them despite the behavior exhibited because of PTSD.

Hopefully, this story will help adults talk with children living with someone who battles PTSD. It can be read to siblings together, a group of children with shared experiences, or just one child alone. Each person's challenges with and reactions to this struggle is unique. While reading this with a child, stop as often as you think necessary and appropriate to ask questions—please refer to the sample questions provided. Especially important is using this story to facilitate a brief explanation of the specific trauma that caused the PTSD or CPTSD related behaviors the child is witnessing—in an age-appropriate manner, of course. Above all, while reading this story, be open to the child's questions and reaction to each part of the story.

This book does not need to be read in one sitting. Feel free to gauge your reading and questions/answers to the child's interest and desire to know more. The discussion between Samuel and his mom and also Samuel and Samantha may be an appropriate place to personalize discussion with your child. It certainly is not necessary to use all the suggested questions or even use them word for word. In fact, pausing with questions and comments too frequently will interrupt the flow of the story. Some questions and comments can be saved for when you discuss or reread the story together.

Remember, most adults do not truly understand this topic, so children will struggle with understanding it as well. However, it is critical that they understand they are loved and nothing is their fault. Finally, like any story, this can be read and reread or referred to in conversations about the child's parent, friend, or relative struggling with PTSD or CPTSD.

All the very best to each of you.

Saturday was my birthday.

Mom had a party for me.

I was so excited until my sister Sarah said, "Dad will ruin it."

"No, he won't," I said.

"Yes, he will," she said.

"No, he won't," I said again. "I've been really good all month.

Last night I told Dad I love him.

He said it back—"I love you too, Samuel."

Aunt Karen, Uncle Bob and my cousins were the first to arrive for my party.

Then some neighbors came and then some friends from school.

After everyone arrived, Dad grilled hot dogs and burgers for us!

Then we had cake, and I opened my presents.

I got electronic games, a remote control car, and some books.

And I got a huge fire truck that had flashing lights and three sirens.

The other kids and I played with it.

The sirens blared, and the lights flashed.

Dad got quiet.

He dropped some plates and spilled his drink.

He ran out of the room.

He drove away in his truck.

Then, everyone else left too.

My sister went to her room.

She always goes to her room when Dad gets upset or mad.

"I told you he'd ruin it!" she yelled before she slammed her door.

Mom cleaned up the mess.

So I went to my room too.

Later, Mom came into my room.

She said she was sorry about what happened.

I said it was okay. "We shouldn't have made so much noise."

Mom said it wasn't my fault.

She said that Dad has something called PTSD.

She told me that his brain was injured or hurt by something bad that happened a while ago.

Things like noises, crowded rooms, and bad dreams upset him because they remind him of what happened back then.

"He can't help it," she said.

"And he feels bad when it happens."

Mom said that he loves us even when he's mad, even when he goes away for a while.

Mom said she feels sad and lonely when Dad won't talk to us.

I guess I don't understand it all, but at least now I know for sure he loves me.

The next day, Samantha, a girl at school, asked me how my party was.

"It was great," I said. "Everybody was there. And I got lots of presents."

I knew Samantha could tell I was sad.

She didn't say anything though.

When I got home from school, I cleaned my room.

I wanted to make Dad happy.

I thought of quiet games I could play when he came home.

Maybe I could just stay in my room like Sarah does.

Dad didn't come home for dinner.

Mom said he was at work, but we knew he wasn't.

I watched TV until it was time to go to bed.

Dad came home two days later.

He said he was sorry for leaving my party.

I said I was sorry we made so much noise.

Mom hugged me.

Then Sarah and I went to the park while Mom and Dad talked.

I asked Sarah what PTSD is. She didn't want to talk about it.

Maybe she didn't really understand either.

One day Samantha's mom called my mom.

She said that she had to go on a little trip.

She asked if Samantha could stay with us for the day.

My mom said, "Sure."

When she came to our house, Samantha seemed sad.

She was quiet and didn't want to play anything.

Mom told me to be nice.

We watched a stupid movie about princesses.

When the movie was over, I got some ice cream.

I asked Samantha what was wrong.

She said, "Mom is sick."

"How?" I asked.

"She has PTSD."

"What?" I said. "She what?"

"She has PTSD," Samantha repeated.

"My dad does too," I said. "But Mom said he's not sick."

"She told me his brain got hurt. She said it makes him feel scared or mad sometimes."

Samantha just looked at me. Then she said, "What do you do when he is mad or scared?"

"I try to be really good," I said, "and very quiet."

I told Samantha I didn't know how to fix Dad.

I told her I tried hard not to upset him.

Samantha said she did the same thing, but nothing ever worked.

I didn't know Mom was listening.

She came into the room and sat down between us.

She talked about PTSD and how it wasn't our fault.

She said that different traumas or bad things that happen could cause PTSD. She asked Samantha about her mom, but Samantha didn't want to talk about it.

I told Mom we were going to play at the park.

At the park, we sat on the swings.

We didn't swing; we just sat there.

Samantha said, "Samuel, maybe nothing is our fault."

I asked, "What do you mean?"

"Well," she said, "if your dad is the same way my mom is, and everyone tells us they have PTSD, maybe they do. And maybe it's really not our fault."

"Does that mean we can't make them change?" I asked Samantha.

"Maybe not," she answered.

We swung on the swings before we went back to my house.

"I'm glad we hung out together today," Samantha said when her mom came to pick her up.

"Do you like to play checkers?" I asked. "Maybe next time we can play checkers."

"Sure," she said. "We have a pool. Maybe someday you can come over."

Then we said goodbye.

After that day Samantha and I spent a lot of time together.

They called us the two Sams, so I had a new name— Sam.

Sometimes we talked, but mostly, we just had fun.

Sometimes Samantha's mom took us places; and sometimes my dad played with us.

Sometimes even Sarah played with us.

One day, when Sarah and I were having breakfast with Mom,

I said, "I still don't understand PTSD."

"None of us kids do," said Sarah.

I thought about that for a minute.

Then I said, "Maybe when I get older I will."

Mom smiled and said, "Maybe not completely, Sam."

And she hugged us both.

Sample Questions

Please use any questions here you think may be helpful or use those of your own.

1. Why do you think Dad left the birthday party?

2. Why did Sarah always go to her room?

3. Does Samuel's dad remind you of anybody you know—your dad, mom, aunt, or grandparent?

4. Did Mom explain PTSD well enough to Samuel? What else might Samuel want to know? Is there anything you want to know?

5. Why didn't Sarah want to talk with Samuel about PTSD?

6. What did Samuel and Samantha decide about their parents and PTSD at the park?

7. Why do you think Samantha and Samuel became friends?

8. At the end of the story, what did Mom mean by "Maybe not completely, Sam."

9. Why do you think Mom hugged Sam and Sarah?

PTSD Basics

By Welby O'Brien

PTSD Is:

Post-Traumatic Stress Disorder can affect anyone, and it results from exposure to an experience that is horrific or life threatening. The whole person gets locked into emergency mode (fight or flight or freeze survival!) and will always be permanently programmed in that emergency mode at some level for the rest of their lives. 24/7 they live as if the original trauma or an impending crisis could occur at any moment. It totally overwhelms their ability to cope so when something triggers them back into survival mode, they have no reserve with which to handle it.

PTSD affects millions just in the U.S. alone, along with all those who love them and care about them.

Because the trauma can impact them on every level (physically, emotionally, mentally and spiritually), the manifestations are quite extensive. Some typical symptoms may include flashbacks, intrusive thoughts of the trauma, avoidance, numbing, putting up walls, withdrawing, hypervigilance, irritability, easily startled, memory blocks, sudden bursts of anger or other emotions, difficulty sleeping, nightmares, fear, depression, anxiety, substance abuse and other addictive behaviors, difficulty holding a job, relationship problems, and unfortunately sometimes even suicide. (See www.LoveOurVets.org for more information.) They are people who are reacting normally to an abnormal experience.

PTSD is NOT:

Post-Traumatic Stress Disorder is not a chosen situation, an illness, a temporary condition, nor is it 100% curable. People who struggle with it are not crazy, weak, failures, bad people, nor are they without help and hope. They can learn to thrive again!

PLEASE DON'T:

Don't pity them.
Don't fear or avoid them.
Don't try to "fix" them.
Don't judge.
Don't assume you know what they are going through.
Do NOT say:
Aren't you over it yet?
You are crazy.
Just get over it.
It's all in your head.
Just be stronger.
I have a total cure for you.
At least you weren't wounded.
I had that but I got over it.
What you really need to do is ____.
You're on your own now.
Pull yourself together.
It's all in the past.
Suck it up.
Move on.

PLEASE DO:

Treat them with kindness and respect.
Acknowledge the depth and reality of their struggle.
Encourage and support them.
Try to imagine a day and night in their shoes.
Accept that you will never fully understand.
Invite them to explore resources together if they want.
Respect their need for space.
Offer to go with them to a local Vet Center, VA, doctor, or counselor.
Be supportive of the loved ones.
Pray for them.
Listen to them.
Love them.
Realize that with PTSD every day is a victory.

This information is intended to provide a brief summary. Do not use it to diagnose or treat any condition. Please consult a qualified health or mental health care provider.

www.LoveOurVets.org

www.PTSDProjects.com

© Welby O'Brien, author of LOVE OUR VETS: Restoring Hope for Families of Veterans with PTSD

Made in the USA
Lexington, KY
29 November 2018